Edwin Jaquett Sellers

Captain John Avery

President Judge at the Whorekill in Delaware Bay, and his Descendants

Edwin Jaquett Sellers

Captain John Avery
President Judge at the Whorekill in Delaware Bay, and his Descendants

ISBN/EAN: 9783337087975

Printed in Europe, USA, Canada, Australia, Japan

Cover: Foto ©Raphael Reischuk / pixelio.de

More available books at **www.hansebooks.com**

Captain John Avery

President Judge
at the
Whorekill
in
Delaware Bay
and his
Descendants

By

Edwin Jaquett Sellers

Philadelphia
MDCCCXCVIII

PRESS OF
J. B. LIPPINCOTT COMPANY,
PHILADELPHIA.

Introduction

For account of Captain John Avery's descendants, see "Kollock Genealogy," by the writer, printed 1897.

For English Avery references, see "The Genealogist's Guide," by George W. Marshall, last edition; for reference to John Avery, the Pirate, see "Dictionary of National Biography," edited by Sidney Lee.

For American Avery references, see Munsell's "Index to American Genealogies," last edition; "The Dedham Branch of the Avery Family in America," published by Winslow W. Avery, 1893; and "The Averys of Groton," by Homer De Lois Sweet, 1894.

The following are the only references I have found to any Avery settlers in Virginia. There were Averys there at a later period who may have been descendants of this settler.

The "Virginia Magazine of History and Biography," Vol. II., p. 181:

Abstracts of Virginia Land Patents.

"(101) Jacob Averie (lease for 21 years) 500 acres on Skiff's Creek (Warwick County), extending northerly 'towards the Creek towards Martin's Hundred,' Southwest towards the land of Thomas Nowell, and East towards the maine—beginning on the east side of a spring called Jacob's Well—1630—By Sir John Harvey."

P. 185:

"(109) Thomas Harwood, of Skiffes Creek, gentleman, 140 acres on Skiffes Creek abutting southerly on the land of M^m Avery. Due in right of Hugh Heyward made over to him June 20, 1631—By Harvey, September 1, 1632."

"(110) John Pott, of Harrop, within the Corporation of James City, doctor in Physick, 200 acres on Skiffes Creek, adjoining the lands of Mr Thomas Nowell and Mr Jacob

Avery. Due for the adventure of four servants: John Mil-
ward, Randolph Holt, Ruth a maid servant, and Thomas
Popkin—By Harvey, Sep. 1, 1632."

P. 311:

"(137) Jacob Averie, gentleman, lease of 500 acres on
Skiffes Creek, 250 thereof stretching northerly towards the
creek towards Martin's Hundred, Southwest towards the
lands of Thomas Nowell, &c. (one of the line marks named is
a spring called Jacob's Well), and the other 250 lying at the
head of said Creek—By Harvey, February 2, 1630—(sic)."

The following references to Avery settlers in Maryland
are abstracted from the Records of the Land Office at Annapolis, and are here given without any attempt to suggest
the relationship to each other or to Captain John Avery.

Liber X, folio 173:

"John Avery * of Maryland, Mariner, has patented 300
acres out of a warrant of 500, Sep. 22, 1658, lying on the
North side of Cuttance, Manor of Nanticoke. Recorded
1666."

Liber VI, fol. 85:

"I George Barrett do assign over unto Thomas Bradley
Esq or his assignes all my right and Title of land due to me
for transporting into this Province: Cornelius Jones, who
came in the year 1650, myself 1650, Francis Stone 1654,
John Avery † 1657, Mark Davenport, 1660, Richard Coger
1658, Abraham Clark, 1654, Witness my hand this 4ᵗʰ October 1663.

Signum
GEORGE B BARRETT

Test:

RICHᴰ FOSTER
Signum
SUSAN X TUCKER"

* This was John Avery, of Dorchester, whose will is hereafter given.
† This may have been either Captain John Avery or the John Avery,
of Dorchester, whose will is hereafter given.

Liber XII, fol. 381 :

" 1669—December the 16ᵗʰ Came *John Avery* * of Calvert County and proved right unto one hundred & fifty acres of land being due to him for transporting into this Province himself and his daughter *Ann*, and William Johnson his servant, to inhabite

Warrant then issued in the name of the said John Avery for 150 acres of land being due to him for the consideracon above said.

Cert. retᵇˡ 16ᵗʰ March next."

Liber XII, fol. 513 :

" These may certifie that I *Edward Avery* do assign all my right of land due to me for my servitude in this provivince unto John Gibbs of the County of Baltimore, planter.

Witness my hand and seale this 31ˢᵗ of October 1668

his
EDWARD ✕ AVERY
mark

Signed and sworne ⎫
unto before me ⎬
JOHN COLLET" ⎭

Liber XI, fol. 104 :

" Know all men by these presents that I Charles James of Baltimore County, Gent., have assigned, and by these presents do assign unto Thomas Godlington of London, merchant all my right, title and interest due to me upon record for the transportacon of John Foster, Richard Leake, Stephen Harper, Thomas Price, *Edward Avery*, Giles Porter, . . . Witness my hand the xiiᵗʰ day of October Annoq. Domini MDCLxvii

C. JAMES [SEAL]"

Liber XII, fol. 351 :

" October xxiˢᵗ Mdclxix Came George Beckwith and proved right to three hundred acres of land for transporting himself, Johannah Porter, *Henry Avery*, John Watts, Thomas Weeke & Thomas Stevens here to inhabite."

* This is the same John Avery, of Dorchester, whose will is hereafter given.

Liber XVII, fol. 574:

" Decr 23^d 1678 *William Avery* of St. Marys County proved right to fifty acres of land for his time of service performed in this province. Assigned said right to Thomas Courtney of same county"

Liber XII, fol. 554:

" June the fourth 1670 Came Henry Hosier of the County of Calvert, Mcht. and proved right unto 1050 acres of land it being due to him for transporting these persons following into this Province to inhabite. Vizt: William Key, *John Avery,** *Vertu Avery* (and 21 others)"

Liber XV, fol. 332:

"January 24, 1675 Came *Virtue Avery* of St. Marys County and proved her right to Fifty acres of land for her time of service performed in this province to Thomas Griffin"

Liber XV, fol. 344:

" Know all men by these presents that I, *Vertue Avery* for a valuable consideration do hereby assign over unto Michael Rockford my right to fifty acres of land due to me for my time of service performed in this province. To have and to hold the same unto him the said Michael Rockford his heirs and assigns forever

Witness my hand and seal this 24th of January 1675

Signum

Test : VERTUE × AVERY

—— PAINTER"

Liber XXII, fol. 337:

" *Robert Avery.*

Cert. 240 acres called ' Unpleasant' 1685."

Liber XXII, fol. 355:

" Cert 160 acres called 'Teagues Content' 1688." (This refers to the same Robert Avery.)

---

* This may have been either Captain John Avery or the John Avery, of Dorchester, whose will is hereafter given.

Liber IX, fol. 120 :
" *Arthur Avery*
Cert. 100 acres called ' Chance' 1665"

Liber XI, fol. 303 :
" Joseph Avery receives 100 acres called ' Knotting.' "

Liber X, fol. 180–1 :
" To the Honb'le Leiv' Gen^{ll}
A survey had and taken of a parcell of Land for John
Avery * lying and being on the north side of Cuttomactico
beginning at a marked oak dividing it from the land of
Thomas Cottingham called Averys Pollicy from thence
running easterly the breadth of one hundred and fifty pole
to a marked tree, thence running northerly the length of
three hundred and twenty pole to a marked tree, from thence
running westerly the bredth of one hundred and fifty pole
to a marked tree, with a line drawn southerly to the first
bounder. Surveyed and now laid out for three hundred
acres more or less by me March the last, 1666
                              STEVEN HORSI
                              Surveyor Generall
        Attested by me
           JEROME WHITE"

" Cecelius &c To all persons to whom these presents shall
come Greeting in our Lord God everlasting. Know yee
that wee for and in consideracon that John Avery of our
Province of Maryland, Marriner hath due unto him three
hundred acres of Land within our said province out of a
warrant for five hundred acres of land granted to the said
Avery as appears upon record & upon such consideracons
and terms as are expressed in our condicons of Plantacon
of our said Province of Maryland under our Greater Seal,
at armes bearing date at London the second day of July in
the year of our Lord God One thousand six hundred forty-
nine with such alteracons as in them is made by our dee-

---

* Probably John Avery, of Dorchester.

laracon bearing date the two and twentyeth day of September Anno One thousand six hundred fifty-eight and remaining upon record in our said Province of Maryland, Doe hereby Grant unto the said John Avery a parcell of Land called Averys Polliey lying & being on the north side of Cuttamactico begining at a marked oak divideing it from the land of Thomas Cottingham from thence running easterly the bredth of one hundred and fifty pole to a marked tree, thence running northerly the length of three hundred and twenty pole to a marked tree from thence running westerly the bredth of one hundred and fifty pole to a marked tree with a line drawn southerly to the first bounder, containing and laid out for three hundred acres more or less together with all rights proffits and bennefits thereunto belonging Royall mines excepted. To have and to hold the same unto him the said John Avery his heirs and assigns forever to be holden of us and our heirs as of our Mannor of Nanticoke in free and common soccage by fealty only for all manner of services yeilding and paying therefor yeerly unto us or our heirs at our Receipt at St. Marys at the two most usual feasts in the year vizt: at the feast of the Annuncacon of the blessed Virgin Mary and at the feast of St. Michael the Arch angell by even & equall porcons the rent of six shillings sterling in silver or gold and for a fine upon every alienacon of the said land or any part or parcell thereof one whole yeers rent in silver or gold or the full value thereof in such commodities as wee or our heirs or such officer or Officers appointed by us or our heirs from time to time to collect and receive the same shall accept in discharge thereof at the choice of us or our heirs or such officer or officers as aforesaid Provided that if the said John Avery his heirs or assigns shall not pay unto us or our heirs or such Officer or Officers as afores[d] the said sume for a fine before such alienacon and enter the said alienacon upon Record either in the Provinciall Court or in the County Court where the said parcell of land lyeth within one month next after such alienacon the said alienacon shall be void and of none effect. Given at St. Maries under our great seal of our said Province of Maryland this eighth and twentyeth day of September in the five and thirtyeth year of our Dominion over our said province of Maryland Annoq Domini one thousand six hundred sixty six Witness our dear son Charles Calvert Esq. our Lievtenᵗ Generall of our said province of Maryland."

Liber XII, fol. 610 :

" On the backside of a warrant granted unto John Avery of the County of Dorchester for one hundred and fifty acres of land the twelfth day of May 1670 was thus written (vizt :)

Surveyed of this warrant thirty six acres

THOMAS TAYLOR Dep'ʸ Su'rvᵗ.

To the Honbˡ the Suryeyor Generall May the 16ᵗʰ 1670—

By virtue of a warrant granted unto John Avery out of his Ldpps Secretarys Office dated the twelfth day of May, this is in humble manner to certifie that I, Thomas Taylor have laid out a parcell of land on the east side of Chesapeake Bay in a creek called Oyster creek upon the west side of the said creek begining at a marked cedar, for length one hundred seventy five p'ches to a marked pyne thence west south west the bredth of thirty four p'ches to a marked pyne bounding on the west with Oyster creek and a line north north west the length of one hundred seventy five p'ches thence with a paralell line to the first bounded tree containing and now laid out for thirty six acres more or less to be held of the Mannoʳ of Nanticoke

THOMAS TAYLOR, Dep'ʸ Survᵉʳ"

Liber XIV, fol. 107 :

" Cecilius &c. Know yee that wee for and in consideracon that John Avery of the County of Dorchester in our said province of Maryland Planter hath due unto him thirty six acres of land within our said province, part of a warrᵗ for 150 acres to him formerly granted as appears upon record. And upon such conditions and terms as are expressed in our conditions of plantation of our said province of Maryland under our greater seale at Armes bearing date at London the second day of July in the yeer of our Lord God 1649

with such alterations as in them is made by our declaration
bearing date 22ᵈ day of September Anno 1658 and remaining upon record in our said province of Maryland Doe
grant unto him the said John Avery all that parcell of Land
called Averys Lott on the east side of Chesapeake Bay in a
creek called Oyster creek upon the west side of the said
creek, Beginning at a marked cedar, for length of one hundred seventy five p'ches, to a marked pine thence west south
west thirty-four pch'es to a marked pine bounding on
the west with Oyster creek & a line drawn north north
west the length of one hundred seventy five p'ches thence
with a paralell line to the first bounded tree, Containing
and now laid out for 36 acres more or less Together with all
Rights profitts and benefitts thereunto belonging (Royall
Mines Excepted) To have & to hold the same unto him
the said John Avery his heirs & assigns forever to be
holden of us and our heirs as of our mannor of Nanticoke
in free & common soccage by fealty only for all manner
of services—yeilding and paying therefor yearly to us or
our heirs at our Receipt at our Citie of Saint Maries at the
two most usual feasts in the year, vizt. at the feast of the
annunciaton of the blessed Virgin Mary, and at the feast of
St. Michael the archangell by even & equall portions the
rent of 7ᵈ 2ᶠ Sterling in silver or gold, and for a fine upon
every alienation of the said land or any part or parcell
thereof, one whole years rent in silver or gold or the full
value thereof in such commodities as we or our heirs or
such officer or officers appointed by us or our heirs from
time to time to collect or receive the same shall accept in
discharge thereof as the choice of us or our heirs or such
officer or officers as afsᵈ. Provided that if he the said John
Avery his heirs or assigns shall not pay to us or our heirs or
such officer or officers as afsᵈ the said sume for a fine before
such alienation and enter the said alienation upon record
either in the Provincial Court or in the County Court where
the said parcell of land lyeth within one month next after
such alienation, the said alienacon shall be void and of none
effect. Given at our Citie of St. Maries under our great

seal of our said province of Maryland this sixth day of September in the thirty nineth year of our dominion over our said province Annoq. Domini 1670."

Liber XVIII, fol. 54:

" To his Excellency the Cap⁺. Generall August 6, 1674

By virtue of a warrant bearing date the fifth day of August in the 42ˢᵈ year of the Dominion of the Rt. Honᵇˡᵉ Cæcilius Annoq Domini 1673 granted unto John Avery * of Somersett County, marriner, signed by me Francis Jenkins by order and appointment of his Excellency the Capᵗ Generall of this province. These are therefor humbly to certifie that I Francis Jenkins, Deputy Surveyor under the Honorable Baker Brooke Esqʳ, Survʳ Genˡ, have laid out for the said John Avery a parcell of Land called Averys Choice, Scituate, lying and being on the seaboard side near Dellaware Bay about four miles from the Whorekill on the east side of a bay called Rehoboth bay, bounded as followeth, Beginning at a marked white oak standing upon a point of land at the mouth of a small creek called Island creek, thence with a line drawn west by north for bredth up the said Rehoboth Bay ninety p'ches to a marked white oake stake sett up in a marsh near the bounded tree on the south side of a parcell of land surveyed for John Walker, thence with a line drawn north by east for length five hundred thirty three perches and one third part of a perch to a marked oake thence by a line drawn East by south ninety perches to a marked Red oake standing on the south side of a branch, and from thence with a right line drawn to the first bounder, Containing three hundred acres more or less To be holden of the Mannor of Worcester

FRANCIS JENKINS

Depty Survᵗ."

Rent Rolls, Soms⁺ & Dorchʳ No. 1, fol. 26:

" 300 acres Averys Pollicy, Sur. 31, Mch. 1666, for *John Avery* on the North side of Cuttomactico at a marked oak

* The same John Avery as before, of Dorchester.

dividing it from the land of Thomas Cottingham. The Land Poss' is included in a survey of 480 a.ᵈ for Wᵐ Elgett by Spe¹ warrᵗ."

Rent Rolls Somst. & Dorchᵣ No. 1, fol. 223:

"300 acres Averys Choice, Sur. 6ᵗʰ August, 1673 for *John Acery* on the seaboard side near Dellaware Bay about 4 miles from the Whorekill on the East side Rehoboth Bay as before.

The Whorekill's not in this Co'ty."

Reg. of Wills, Annapolis, Md.
Liber A, 1676–1677, fol. 199:
"In the name of God, Amen.

I, *John Avery* of the County of Dorchester in the Province of Maryland, ship-wright, now being in perfect memory although somewhat indisposed in bodily health—praised be God Almighty do make & ordaine this to be my last will & testament.

Impᵃ: I will and bequeath my soule to God that gave it in perfect hope by Christ Jesus my Redeemer to be saved by his onely merits and my body to the earth from whence it came, by decent buriall.

Secondly: I will and bequeath all my real estate in the County of Dorchester unto my well-beloved wife Anne during her naturall life and after her decease unto my grandson John Granger and his heirs forevermore.

Thirdly: I will and bequeath unto my said beloved wife Anne all and every part and parcell of my personall estate whatever chattells, moveables, bonds bills, accompts or whatsoever unto me may personally belong or appertaine in every respect, unto her and her heirs for ever, after my debts are paid and funerall charges satisfied.

Lastly: I will and bequeath that my said beloved wife Anne be my full and sole executrix of this my last will and testament, and she doe take care of my said grand child John Granger, hereby making null and void all other wills and testaments and codicills whatever formerly by me made, and published This to be my last will and testament.

Signum

JOHN A AVERY [SEAL]

Published, sealed and de-
clared in the presence of
GEORGE TAURY
THOS PATTISON
Signum
MARY × MEREDITH
Signum
MARY × JANES

Proved in common forme
April 21, 1677."

From Register of St. Mary Ann's Parish, Cecil Co., Md.:
"Litan Leeds Kimble was married to *Mary Avery* the 22ᵈ day of January 1675. He was born July 27ᵗʰ 1747"
"*Mary Avery*, daughter of *Peter & Elijah* (?) *Avery* was born October 8ᵗʰ 1744."

1 Pa. Col. Rec., p. 549–580—Capt. John Avery, the pirate.

Pa. Mag., Vol. V, p. 175—Capt. John Avery, the pirate.

The following is copied from an old poem in possession of Mr. Charles R. Hildeburn, of Phila.
At the top of the poem is a picture of a three-masted ship under full sail.

BOLD CAPTAIN AVERY

Come all ye young Sailors of courage so bold,
That venture for money, I'll cloth you with gold.
Come resort unto Broney, and there you will find,
A ship call'd the Fanny will pleasure your mind.

Bold Avery commands her and calls for his own,
And he'll box her about before he has done:
French, Spaniards, Portuguese, and Heathens likewise
He has made war with them till the day that he dies.

She's rigg'd and man'd, and most neatly trim'd,
She's model'd like wax-work and sails with the wind.
She has all things in order fit for our design,
God prosper the Fanny, she's bound for the main.

Farewel to the Plymouth, Catwater be damn'd,
For once I was owner of part of this land;
But since I'm disowned, Adieu I will take
My person from England my fortune to make.

I'll cross the South Seas with courage so bold,
For my men I resolve to cloath them with gold;
Five hundred and fifty brave boys of courage,
Resolve the first ship they meet to engage.

The Northerly climate is now fit for me,
I'll cross the Tropicks that all men may see
That I'm not afraid to let the world know,
I'll cross the seas, and to Persia will go.

I'll honor St. George and his Colours I'll bear,
Good quarters I'll give you, but no nations spare;
For the world must supply me if ever I want,
I'll give them my fill when my money grows scant.

Lo this is the Course I intend for to steer,
They that honor St. George the better shall fare,
For he that refuses shall surely soon spy,
Strange Colours on board my Fanny to fly.

Three shivers of gold, with a red flow'ry Field,
Embroidered with Gold, that shall be our shield,
So call for your quarter as soon as you can see,
Our bloody flag hoisted, this is our decree.

No quarter I'll give, no quarter I'll take,
There is no one man living, one glass is too late;
For we are sworn brothers, and it is my design,
I'm bound for the Indies, the gold shall be mine.

Now this is the Course I intend for to steer,
My hard-hearted nation to you I declare;
I have done you no wrong, so you may me forgive,
For my sword shall maintain me as long as I live.

My commission is large, for I made it myself,
My captain may stretch it wider by half;
'Twas dated at Croney, believe me, my friend,
In the year ninety-two boys unto my life's end."

Captain John Avery

I. 1. CAPTAIN JOHN AVERY was undoubtedly of English origin, but when or where he was born is unknown. The first reference to him, with certainty, is the following:

Land Office, Annapolis, Md.
Liber VII, fol. 580:
" June vi, 1665—John Avery enters rights himself, Sarah his wife, Francis Raines, Edward Perkins, this year. Warrant dated ut supra, Retbl vi^th December next for two hundred acres."

From this reference we are unable to determine when John Avery came here, for it frequently happened that land was not claimed until several years after settlement. It may be, therefore, that the above John Avery is one of those referred to in the Introduction; he may have come here at one of the dates there mentioned and afterwards have gone to Virginia or elsewhere, married, and brought his wife back to Maryland with him. The writer believes such to have been the case, although, for certainty, he has decided to begin the account of Captain John Avery with the reference to his claiming rights in 1665. His wife's surname has not been ascertained, which is probably due to his having married without the Province of Maryland.

Although he claimed two hundred acres, the writer has been unable to find that he received them; he may have assigned his rights before settling in Delaware.

It has not been ascertained when he moved to Delaware; the first reference to him there is the following:

Deeds, Georgetown, Del.

Book 2, p. 288 :

" Edmund Andross Esq., Seigneur of Sausmare etc. . . . .
Certain parcell or tract of land near unto Whore Kill in
Delaware Bay called " Avery's Rest," lying upon Rehoboth's
Bay. The said John Avery to pay therefor yearly Quit Rent
of 8 bushels of good winter wheat.

Signed 15 Jan. 1675, EDMUND ANDROSS—MATHIAS NICH-
OLLS, Dep."

Pa. Ar., Sec. Ser., Vol. V, p. 690 :

" Commission of John Avery as Captain by Sir Edmund
Andros.

EDMOND ANDROS Esq'. &c.

By virtue of his Majesties Letters Patents, and the Cômission and authority unto me given by his royal Highness,
I do hereby in his Maties Name, constitute and appoint you
John Avery to be a Captain of the Foot Company, of the
Militia at the Whore Kill; You are therefore carefully
to perform the Duty of a Captain, in all Things, and to
observe such orders, as you shall from time to time receive
from me, or other your Superior Officer, and all other Inferior Officers and Soldiers of the said Company, are to obey
you as their Captain, according to the Discipline of Warr,
This Cômission to be of force for the space of one whole
Year or till further Order.

Given under my Hand and Seal in New York, this 26th
day of October 1676.

                                        E : ANDROS."

From N. Y. Col. MSS., Vol. XXI, p. 8.   In N. Y. State
Library, Albany, N. Y.:

" To the Honorable EDMOND ANDROSS Esqr Capt. Gen^ll of
all his Royall Highnes Territoris in America.

Whereas it was yor Honor^s good pleasure to put and Con-
signe mee though a p^rson unworthy of soe high a Calling
to bee a magistrate at the whorekilles in which office &
Calling I have Indeavored by the help of god to discharge

my Conscience before god and man to the best of my skill
and knowledge without favor or Affection to any prson and
for soe Doeing I have received many Abuses both from Mr.
John Avery and Mr. Henry Smith and for noe other Cause
nor Reason as I know of but for Doeing my office which I
humble Conseave to bee my Duty to Doe when Lawfull
Called thereto by any of his majesties subjects and not to be
called Roague and beggerly Roague with many such like
abusesive Speatches Saieing Sarra you pettyfull Lousy Ras-
kell Lett mee know you ever grant any Atteachm' or war-
rants againe and you had better be hanged and if the Governor Doth Lett Such pettifull Raskels to bee in Commission
I will not Sitt for I hold it beneath mee to sitt with such a
pettyfull fellow as thou art. It is not onely mee but others
of the Comission when they will not bee Conformable to
his unreasonable will for Mr. John Kiphaven because he
would not Draw him a Bottell of Rom for a Indian hee had
hired on the Sabbath Day In the Like termes and for noe
other Cause that I know of unreasonably abused by Mr.
John Avery And as for Mr. Henry Smith his Abuses to the
Court and the book of Lawes are not Inferior to the Rest:
for if wee Doe act any thing Contrary against Mr. Smith
his will then wee are Called Roagues and a Confeaderate
with Roagues and with other treathning words which as I
Humbly Conseave not to bee omitted therefore thought it
my Duty to Informe yo' Honor with it for if I Issue forth a
Sommons or a warrant In His Majesties name to warren In
any persons who are Liveing In Mr. Smith his howse Either
the warrant is not Executed or if Executed not obeyed for
hee Doth pretend they are his Servants and not to Answer
noe warrant or Sommons without his Leave but I Humbly
Conceave though they where Mr. Smith his Servants which
I know not such thing for to my knowledg they were both
freeman not long sence yet they where as Lyable to his
Maties Lawes as Mr. Smith or any other person if they bee
good subjects this being part of the Errigular proceedings I
humble beseech yo' Honor to give mee the patient pers[on]al
hearing hereof for should I take a pennman to writt all it

would weary the hand of a good penn man to writt and yor
Honors Eares to heare an Like yor Honor I have send all
the proceedings that I have Done in my office and place
which I hope yor Honor will peruse and find whither I have
Deserved these Abuses or no and wholy Rely upon yor
Honors good pleasure Either to Justifie mee or condem
mee as yor Honors wisdom shall thinck fitt Soe hoping yor
Honor In yor good time will Rectifie Both these and all
others misdemeanors by whoesoever committed one thing I
humble begg of yor Honor not that I am worthy to give
advise but onely begg it of yor Honor Both for the good of
the people and the good of the place that yor Honor will be
pleased to Constitute Sum wise Discreete sober minded
Gentleman that may Lead the people into obidience for the
safety of a King or Cheife governor Consistes In obidient
people for hee that knowes not how to obey neither knowes
not how to Command for which Cause I humbly Beseech
yor Honor to make Choyse of a Cheife Commander according to yor Honors Discretion for this partes And that yor
Honor will bee pleased to Discharge mee from this and all
other offices of trust which is the humble Request of yor
Honors Servant to Command Soe hopeing yor Honor will
be pleased to pardon my Boldnes and make the best Con-
structions of these my Rude Lines I am and ever shall
Remaine as in Duty bound yor Honors Humble Servant Soe
wishing all health and happiness to Attend yor Honor Both
in this Life and the Life to Com which is the prayer of him
who is yor Honors Humble Servant to Command

                                 EDWARD SOUTHRIN.

From the Whorekill
    Septr 18th Ann° 1676"

Deed recorded at Georgetown, Del.:
"EDMOND ANDROSS Esq; SEIANEUR OF SAUSMAREZ LIEU-
TENANT & GOVERNOUR GENERALL, under his Royall Highness, JAMES, DUKE OF YORK, and ALBANY, & of all his
teritories in AMERICA, to all to whom these Presents shall
come, sendeth GREETING:

WHEREAS, There is a certain tract of land called Martin's Vinyeard lying at the Whorekill on the west side of Delaware Bay, the metts by vertue of a warrant hath been laid out for Henry Stritchor;* Begining at a certain small creek lyeing by a place called Kickout, begining at the point by the Whorekills running & bounding upon the said kill south east in breadth One hundred and fifty perches to a bounded white oak standing upon the point of a marsh, and from thence up the said marsh south west six hundred & forty perches to an other bounded white oak standing by the said marsh and from thence north west bounding upon the woods to a bounded hickory or walnut tree standing by the aforesaid creek one hundred and fifty perches then the said creek to the point in the Whorekill north east six hundred and forty perches, containing and laid out for Six Hundred Acres, as by the return of the survey brought in by Captain Edmond Cantwell, the surveyor doth & may appear. Now for a confirmation unto him the said Henry Stritchor in his possession and enjoyment of the premises; Know ye that by virtue of the commission and authority unto me given by his Royal Highness I have Ratified Confirmed & Granted and by these Presents do ratify confirm and grant unto the said Henry Stritchor, his heirs and Assigns the aforesaid parcel of land and premises. With all and Singular, the Appurtenances to have and to hold the said parcel of land and premises unto the said Henry Stritchor his heirs and assigns unto the proper use and behoof of the said Henry Stritchor his heirs and assigns forever. He continueing in obediance and conforming himself according to the laws of the Government. And yeilding and paying therefore yearly and evry year as a quitt rent unto his Royal Highness six bushels of good wintor wheat unto such person or persons there in authority as shal be empowered to receive same.

Given under my hand, and sealed with the seal of the Province in New York, the Twenty fifth day of March in the Twenty Eighth year of his Majesty's reign, Anno Domini, One Thousand Six Hundred and Seventy Six.

* Stretcher.

2

(Recorded by order of the Governor. the day and year above written.)

E. ANDROSS.

Examined by me,
MATTHIAS NICHOLLS, Sec."

" Know all men by these presents that we Henry Stretchor and Sarah Stretchor for a valuable consideration already received do by these presents alienate assign and make over all our right title and interest of this within mentioned patent from us our heirs executors administrators and assigns unto Capt. John Avery his heirs executors administrators and assigns forever.

IN Witness hereof, have hereunto set our hands this 11th. day of Feb. A. D. 1678.

Signed sealed and de-⎫ HENRY STRETCHER   [SEAL].
livered in the presence ⎬   the mark of
of us,   ⎭ SARAH ✕ STRETCHER. [SEAL].

Acknowledged in open court Feb. 11th. 1678.
Test. COM. VERHOOF Clk. Whorekills

Recorded the 2nd. of May 1715. JOHN HEPBURN master of the Rolls. for County of Sussex."

Pa. Ar., Sec. Ser., Vol. V, p. 705 :
" Commission to Capt. John Avery &c. to be Justices at the Whore Kill in Delaware Bay.

SIR EDMUND ANDROS Kᵗ &c. :
By vertue of his Maᵗⁱᵉˢ Letters Pattents & the Cômission and Authority unto me given by his Royal Highness I do hereby in his Maᵗⁱᵉˢ Name Constitute, appoint and Authorize you John Avery, Francis Whitwell, Alexander Molestine, John Kiphaven, Luke Wattson, John Roades, & James Wells to be Justices of the Peace at the Whore Kill and dependences in Delaware Bay and any four or more of you to be a Coᵗ of Judicature And in case of Sickness, absence

or otherwise of ye first &c. The Next in Côrnission to pre-
side Giveing and Granting unto you and every of you full
power to Act in said Employm' according to Law Regu-
lacôn and former practise of which all Persons concerned
are to take Notice & give you the due Respect & Obedience
belonging to your Places in Discharging your Dutyes This
Côrnission to be of force for the space of One Year after the
date hereof and taking your Oathes and Places for the same
or till further Order.

Given under my hand and Seale of the Province in New
York this 8th of October in the 30th Year of his Maties Name
Anog Domini 1678.

E. Andross.

Examined by me

Mathias Nicholls Secr :"

P. 706 :

" Certificate of Capt Avery taking the Oath with power
to Administer to ye rest of ye Bench.

By the Governor :

Whereas you have this day taken your Oath as Magistrate
or Justice of the Peace of the Cort at the Whore Kill in
Delaware Bay for the ensueing Yeare These are in his Maties
Name to Appoint and Authorize you at your Arrival there
to Administer the Oath to the others Joyned wth you in
Côrnission wch done and having taken your Places to act
accordingly.

Given under my hand in New Yorke this 12th day of
Octobr 1678.

Past the office

M : N : Secr."

From N. Y. Col. MSS., Vol. XXI, p. 62. Letter of Luke
Watson :

" Whoore Kill ye 30th June 1679.

Honored Sir

Your Honor hath beene pleased to Joyne me in Common
with others As A Magistrate for this county ; which I have
ever sence bene both willing and readye to sarve you and

my Countrey to the best of my Judgment; And haveing
that Trust reposed in me I look upon myselfe oblidged to
Informe your Honor of such miscarriages and misdemeners
as happen or fall out that Cannot be rectified here; And
that is the Grose Abuses that hath bene Commited by Capt.
John Avery presedent of this Court; both relating to the
Trust reposed in him and other ways;

1ˢᵗˡʸ. That when the rest of the Magistrats could not Con-
sent to doe and determine things as he would have it; Contrary to our Judgment He have in A greate Rage and furey
went out of Court Cursing and swaring; Calling of the rest
of the Court ffooles Knaves and Rouges; wishing that if
ever he satt Amongst us again; that the devil might Com
and fetch him away; and also threeting and presently after
did strik one of the Mgistrats with his Kane; and had he
not bene prevented by the spectators might a done much
damage that way.

2ˡʸ He Tooke upon himselfe to Marry the widdow Claiment
to one Bryant Roseles; without publiquation not withstand-
ing shew . . out aske At Least a Moneth to an other man;
namly Edward Leeke; The which when the said Leeke
hard that she was marryed to another man said . . . . .
before death, And presently . . . . . home, fell sick and in
about forty eight houres after . . . . . Left it on his death
that hur Marrying was the Cause of his . . . . .

3ˡʸ. He took upon him to grant A Licence to marry
daniel Browne to Susan Garland widdow; without any
publiquecation, which Marriage was effected; notwith-
standing it is Generally knowne; or at least, the said daniel
Confesses that he knows no other but that he have a wife
Liveing in England;

4ˡʸ. one Judith the wife of Thomas Davids being sub-
spexted to have stoolen sume goods from severall persions,
the goods being found in hur Custidy; was had in examina-
tion by me; And at ffirst she did Confidently Affirm that
she brought the sd goods out of MaryLand; and that they
ware hur owne Lawfull goods; but she well knowing that
it would be proved to be otherwise did soone Confess that

she ded steele them and from whom; upon hur Confession
I made hur . . . . . iss and commited her to the Custidy
of the Cunstable Till the next Court then following; but
soone After Capt. Avery sent a noote by hur husband to the
Cunstable requiring him to give hur hur Libiurty : threcfeu-
ing both me that had commited hur and the Cunstable that
ded detaine hur soe that the Cunstable being surprised with
fear ded discharge hur out of his Custidy; In short he the
said Capt. Avery is au Incouriger and upholder of dronking-
nes Theeft Cursing swearing and flighting to the Affrighting
Amazing and Terificinge of his Matⁱᵉˢ quiet peacable subjects; whoes grose weeckednes and unhuman Con . . . . .
if a timely stop be not put to it; may Justly be expexted to
bring downe gods Heavy Judgment upon this place.

5ˡʸ. I goeing into the house of Helmainas Wittbanck on
the fifteenth Day of this Instnt June being the Lords day;
where the said Capt. Avery was drounk; whoe soone after
brooke out in a greate Rage and feurey; (without any pro-
vocation); Calling me beagerly Rouge and theefe with maney
more reflexting speaches; saying that he would prove me to
be both Rouge and theefe : and that I was not worth one
grot; I ded tell him that if he would not give me stisfaccon;
for the abusse he had cast upon me; that I would sue him;
To which he replyed; That he would faine see any Mages-
trate that would dare to signe a warrant or sumeanse Against
him; And that what he had said he would not be Account-
able to any Court but onely to the Governer; and that he is
above any power here; soe that the other Commiseners have
Refused to signe A sumeance Against him; he Curses &
swares at such A rate that he flrights all others from doeing
any thing in order to the bringing him to Justice.

. . . . . I could doe no Less . . . . these
things before your . . . . . for the Clearing of myselfe
from haveinge any unity . . . . . such his Abomenable
wicked practices Life and Conversasion.

And my Humble Request unto your Honnor is that you
will be pleased to give such order and dirextions that the
said Capt. Avery may be Compelled to make good his

Charge Against me; or Else to give me such satisfaccon as shall Appeare to you Just and Equiel; which is the thing desiered and Humblee Craved for by your Honnors

Obedeant & flaithfull servant

LUKE WATSON."

(NOTE.—The . . . . . in the above copy signify the loss of letters in the original manuscript where the paper was torn and missing.)

Deeds, Georgetown, Del.

Book A, p. 104:

" Ct. held for the Whore Kill 8 & 9 of April 1679, Commissioners present, Capt. John Avery, Mr Frances Whitwell, Mr Alex. Malleston, Mr John Kipshaven, Mr Luke Watson, Mr John Roads and Mr James Wells. There was granted unto Capt. John Avery 800 acres of land in addition to former grant."

From N. Y. Col. MSS., Vol. XXVIII, p. 109:

" N. Yorke ye 9th of June, 1679.

CAPT. AVERY

I receaved yor I thinck by this Bearer Mr. Peter Groenendyck & Did Direct Capt. nicolls to prepare an order in Answer to ye Several prticulars & some others but not being Done & Capt. nicolls out of towne, Upon the Sayling of said Groenendyck occations this to tell you the Substance or Result, vizt I doe aprove & Confirme yor Choyse & Recomendations of Cornelis Verhoofe to Continue Clarke of the Cort & Bee Surveyor till further order, & Mr. John Vines to bee Sheriffe Giveing Security Dureing this Corts Commission & theres an account of about 40,000 lbs of tobacco for Surveys which I heare is sworne to by Willm Taylor afore Guilem Verplancken & Attested by him as Alderman being Iregularly & Illeagally taken bee void & of none effect & to Remaine as if not Done. I am

yor Affectonate friend

E. ANDROS"

Underneath was written, " True Copic from ye origionall Examined pr mee, JOHN AVERY."

From N. Y. Col. MSS., Vol. XXI, p. 76:

"New Yorke, August 23ᵈ, 1679.

CAPT. JOHN AVERY,

SIR: Capt. Nathaniel Walker having the Last yeare produced a Survey under the hand of Cornelis Verhoofe of a
parcell of Land layd out for him at the whorekill, called
Cedar neck, containing six hundred and eighty acres, the
which was afterwards certifyed by your Coⁿ, upon my
writing to them from the Governour about it: And the sd
Capt. Walker having the Governours Grant of a patent for
the same, hath for the present respited it upon his desire
that there may bee incerted in the sd patent, besides the
number of Acres aforementioned, a certaine Swamp lyeing
in the meddle of Cedar neck, together with the Sand Hills
& pines by the Sea Side, with the Slashes & marshes or
broaken land, betweene the sd neck and the sea, and Reho-
bay bay, and the Indyan Inlett to the Southward, all wch
the Governour is willing to comply with him in, provided it
will bee no prejudice to any towneship or persons seated
thereby & before his voyage to the Eastward, which hee
began this day fortnight, had hee not beene very full of
buisnesse had written to you himselfe, but being prevented,
desired mee to doe it so that my Request to you is that you
will propose it to the Coⁿ & if it will bee no prejudice as
before, that you will with the first opportunitie returne mee
your Result, that Capt. Walker may no longer bee delayed
about his patent, who when he comes to settle amongst you,
will I doubt not, prove a good neighbour & Inhabitant. I
have not farther on this occasion, so subscribe

       Sir,

              Yoᵣ friend and Servant
                     MATTHIAS NICOLLS."

Deed Office, Georgetown, Del.

Book A, p. 106:

"At a Court held Dec. 1679, Capt. John Avery hath
made and acknowledged a deed of conveyance of 300
acres to Levit Collins and John West."

Same page :

" Wᵐ Futcher granted unto Capt. John Avery 'a parcell of land.' (No description.)
Dec. 1679."

Book A, p. 106 :

" At a Court held Dec. 1679, Henry Stretcher and Sarah his wife, for a valuable consideration already rec'd. acknowledged a 'patton' of land unto Capt. John Avery. Recorded May 2, 1715. See Book D, p. 157–159."

York's Books :

" A parcel of land called 'Goulden quartered' patented to Capt. John Avery containing 300 acres, 7 Mar. 1681. CORNELIUS VORHOOFE, Surveyor. Certified by LUKE WATSON."

Deed Book No. 1, p. 10. Georgetown, Del. :

" Warrant given April 16, 1682 to Capt. John Avery for the Island in Rehoboth Bay upon which he now lives, to be added thereto. The Court approve."

Reg. of Wills, Georgetown, Del. :

Will of Edward Boothe of Deal County. Bequest of 300 pounds of tobacco to Mʳ Avery. Will dated 1682.

Pa. Ar., Sec. Ser., Vol. XVI, p. 369 :

" Oct. 29, 1682. From the Records in Sussex County. The entry of a notification, signed William Penn, dated at Upland, and directed to William Clarke, Luke Watson, John Roads, John Avery, Halmanus Wiltbank, and Alexander Molistone ; he notifies them, that the Duke of York had, by Feoffment, dated 24 Aug. 1682, past and conveyed to him, from 12 miles Southward of New Castle upon Delaware River, to Cape Henlopen, together with the Powers and Jurisdictions thereunto belonging, reserving unto himself one Moyety of the Rent thereof, whereby the said Wil-

liam Penn becomes, also, Proprietary and Governor of the
before-mentioned Tract of Land; He desires them to meet
him, next Thursday, at the Town of Newcastle, being the
2d of November, where he intends to hold a General Court
for the settling the Jurisdiction of these, and your Parts, in
which they will oblige him. If there be any Persons of
Note, or others, that desire to be present, they may come
freely, which you are desired to communicate. Sussex
Records, N° 17. Fol. 16."

(The foregoing was part of the evidence used in the
case of Penn v. Baltimore.—E. J. S.)

P. 370:
"Nov. 7, 1682. From the Records in Sussex County.
Commission from William Penn Esq; dated in New Castle,
whereby he, as Proprietary, and Governor of Pensilvania,
Newcastle, St. Jones, Whorekill alias New Deal, with their
proper Liberties, does, in the King's Name, constitute Luke
Watson, William Clark, John Roads, John Avery, and
Halmanus Wiltbank, or any three of them, to be Justices of
the Peace, and Court of Judicature for the County of
Whorekill alias New Deal; this Commission to be in Force
for one Year, or till further Order. Sussex Records, N° 17,
Fol. 17."

(Evidence in Penn v. Baltimore.)

"Records of the Court of Sussex County, Delaware,"
from the old Court Docket in possession of the Pa. His. Soc.

P. 104:
" April 1682 the Court grant unto Capt. John Avery the
island lying in Rehouer Bay, adjoining unto the land that
the said Capt. Auery * now lives upon and to be surveyed
and added to his land he lives on. Wart. given out the
16th instant."

* In the old spelling the letter u was frequently used for v.

P. 129 :

" Wm Penn's Commission of the Peace Nov 7, 1682. Luke Wattson, William Clark, John Roades, John Aurey and Halmanus Wiltbank, to be Justices."

P. 130 :

" Record of the oath subscribed to by the above commissioned justices on the 14th of Nov. 1682. John Avery did not sign."

P. 144 :

" Court held 9th 10th 11th 11th Mo. 1682.

John Auery, plf. $\Big\}$
Richard Harvey, deft.

The suit falls by the death of the plf. who departed this life the 16th $\frac{mo}{9}$ 1682."

P. 166 :

" Ct. held 13 & 15, $\frac{mo}{12}$ 1682.

Sarah Aurey, plf.,
     administratrix to $\Big\}$ In Action of Trasspasse.
     Capt Jo. Auery, deceased,
Richard Harvey, deft.

The plf. not appearing to present her suit and the deft. crauving an non suit the Court order an non suit to be entered Agt. the plf. with Costs of suit. Als. Execution cod. die."

P. 168 :

" Sarah Auery, Administratrix
     of the Estate of Capt. John Avery, $\Big\}$ An action of
     deceased, plf.   the case."
William Traford, deft.

P. 171 :

" Hercules Sheepard, petitioner.

The petitioner sets forth by his petition that Capt. John Auery, deceased, did before the petitioner was joined in

marriage with Mary, the wife of the petitioner and daughter
of the said Capt. Auery, [say] that he would give unto your
petitioner with his daughter a certain parcell or tract of
land which was late in the occupation of Thomas Davids,
together with the plantation, house & premises thereunto
belonging, which said land Lyes Between the land of John
Depree and the land that the widow Auery now lives upon,
and that the said John Auery did after the said marriage
was solemized give your petitioner possession of the said
land and premises; and that he did declare the same when
he lay upon his death bed and proved the same by the testi-
mony of several witnesses. The Court, taking the same
into their consideration and several members of the Court
having themselves heard the said John Auery say that his
daughter Mary should have the said land, the Court,
therefore, pass their judgment that the land do properly
belong unto the petitioner and his heirs and assigns forever."

P. 172:
"Eodie. Upon the petition of Sarah Auery, the administratrix of John Auery deceased, the Court is pleased to
remit and forgive the fine of the said John Auery that is as
yet unpaid, being nine hundred and fifty pounds of tobacco."

P. 204:
"15th 6 mo. 1683.
The Court ordered the appraisers of Capt. Auery's Estate
should appraise it as it was when he died as near as could
be and if any of the 4 appraisers be wanting, they may
choose another in his place, and that John Roads shall swear
them for the true appraising thereof."

From N. Y. Coll. MSS., Vol. XXI, p. 127:
"To the Right Honnor^{ble} EDMOND ANDROS Governor Gen-
erall over ye nord^n parts in Ameryca.
The humble Peticon of Pet^r Groenendyck sheweth
That Whereas yor peticon^r att ye Whorekill hes obtained
on order against Capt John Avery for ye sume of Lb23:

01ˢ: 7½ᵈ: in money & 2116 pounds of tobacco for ye wich sd sume of money & tobacco Execution was Granted & served upon sume of sd Capt. Avery his astate & preased, but so it is yt sd goods is preased so extrordinary onreasonably as yoʳ honnor if please by ye Proceedings thereof may see so yt yoʳ peticioner should bee a greate Looser thereby.

There for yoʳ Peticionʳ humbly Requests yoʳ honnʳ will be pleased to take this in his Cerius Consideration & to Grant yoʳ peticionʳ on order yt ye sd goods may be sould att a pub-like outcry or other ways yt ye preasers may be compelled to keepe ye sd Goods at ye prise as it is prased . . them & yt yoʳ peticionʳ may have his Just due According to ordʳ & so yoʳ peticionʳ shall pray for Ever."

From N. Y. Coll. MSS., Vol. XXVI, p. 102:

" At a Genˡˡ Coᵗ of Assizes held in New Yorke begin-ning the 3ᵈ & ending the 5ᵗʰ day of October (1677).

Peter Groenendyke plt   John Aver & Henry Smith defts.

The plt having at the last Coᵗ of Assizes made Compˡᵗ agˢᵗ the Coᵗ & Jury at the Whorekill that they had not done him justice in an action depending there between the plt & Henry Smith one of the defts alleadging the presidᵗ to bee a party agˢᵗ him or Attorney to the sd Smith & producing under the hand of 6 of the Jury that they were misled in the case, severall matters being then alleadged of want of proofe, & Henry Smith not appearing, The case was referred to this Coᵗ where none of ye defts but Henry Smith being present whose excuse for non attendance on ye last Coᵗ was admitted, & pleading not to have had Legall Sumons, or a declaracon delivered in agˢᵗ him now according to Law, The Coᵗ doth dismisse the Cause & order the Action to bee devided, That is to say the plt in one Action to prosecute the Coᵗ & Jury & in another shall prosecute the sd deft Smith by way of Appeale at the next Genˡˡ Cort of Assize.

It is likewise ordered that Evidence taken in open Coᵗ at the Whorekill relating to this matter shall bee admitted in this Coᵗ as valed. And the plt & deft are both to put in security the one to prosecute & the other to make answer at the Co^n aforesd.

By order of ye Co^n of Assizes."

From N. Y. Col. MSS., Vol. XXVI, p. 103:

" At a Gen^{ll} Co^n of Assize . . . . .

Peter Groenendyke Plt   John Avery & Henry Smith, defts.

In the case betweene the Plt & Defts brought into this Co^n by way of Appeale from the verdict & Judgment of the Co^n at Whorekill in Delaware, wherein the Plt taxeth both Co^n & Jury for acting contrary to law & Justice in a suite depending betweene him & Henry Smith one of the defts:

The matter being debated in Co^n & it being alleadged that severall evidences & Copies of ye Co^n Records were wanting, which if time were given might bee produced & the sd Henry Smith one of the Defts though served with the order for his Appearance being absent: It is ordered That the farther hearing of the Case bee remitted until th. . . . . . Gen^{ll} Co^n of Assize to bee held in . . . . . city when all partyes concerned are to appeare, & bring their farther proofes & evidences with them.

The Costs & Charges of this Co^n to bee pd by Henry Smith by reason of his non-appearance unlesse hee shew good Cause to the Governor for the same, which if hee doe, then to bee pd by the plt.

By order of the Gen^{ll} Co^n of Assizes."

(Endorsed 1677.)

From N. Y. Col. MSS., Vol. XXI., p. 122:

" Att A Called Court Held for the Whoore Kill the first day of May Anno Dm. 1680;

Commissioners { Mr. Alexander Moulston { Mr. Luke Wattson } psent.
             { Mr. John Kiphaven   { Mr. James Wells }

Peter Groundik plt   }
Capt. John Avery deft.   }

Whereas the deft the last Court Appealed from the verdict of the Jurey; the deft In psuance for the Judgmt to

the said verdict of the Jurey given In the last Court upon
A defferance then depending betweene this plt and this deft,
of which verdict the deft then Appealed, the Court therefor
hath Excamined the Matter of the proceedings from the
last Court and pass Judgment to be entered Against the
deft to pay forthwith According to the verdict of the Jurey
being the sume of Two Thousand one hundred and sixteene
pounds of Tobacco and lb23 : 00s : 7½d of money, one shill
of dammages with Cost of suite Alias Exemtion and the
bonds passed for the prossecution and Answering the said
Appeal from the order of the last Court to be void and
surrendered to each party; and if the deft be Agreeved of
this Judgment may if please entry Appeale to the Honnor-
able Governor & Councell According to Law;

Test CORNELOUS VERHOOFE Cler.

A True Coppie taken & examined. pr. WM. CLARK."

Extracts from the old Court Docket of Sussex County,
Delaware, in possession of the His. Soc. of Pa., p. 53 :
"14, and 15, June 1681.

The differences that are depending between Capt. John
Avery and Peter Groundyk concering the account of Capt.
Avery overcharging the said Peter Groundyk, it is ordered
and agreed by both the said parties that it shall be referred
to two men to be by them chosen to end and determine, as
also what is once charged in the said Peter Groundyk's
account to Capt. John Avery; and the charges of the Suit
that was this day tried between them to be paid equally by
them; and both persons to enter into bond, the one to the
other of one hundred pounds . . . to stand to the award of
the two men to be chosen."

P. 57.   Same date :
"Henry Bowman, plf. ⎱
Joseph Browne, deft. ⎰ An action of Debt.

The deft. being out of the Government and his attorney,
Capt. John Avery, being sick, petitions the Court for a ref-

erence; the Court, therefore, grants the deft. a reference until the next Court."

Same page and date:
"Henry Bowman, plf.
Andrew Depree and } An action of Debt."
  Joseph Browne, defts.
Entry as above.

"Joseph Browne &
  Andrew Depree, plffs. } An action of Debt."
Henry Bowman, deft.
Entry same as above.

P. 58.   Same date:
"Thomas Howard & Wright
      Howard, plffs. } Action of Trespass."
  Nathaniel Walker, deft.
Entry same as above.

"Andrew Draper, plf.
Thomas Denison, deft. } Action of the Case."
Entry same as above.

"Capt. John Avery, plf.
Benjamin Coudrey, deft. } Attachment."
Entry as above.

P. 59.   Eodie:
"Francis Gunby, plf.
Capt. John Avery, deft. } Action of the Case."
Entry as above.

P. 62:
"Capt. John Avery, plf.
Peter Grundyk, deft. } Plea upon the Case."

" In June Court last it was Refered by Agreement of the plf. and the deft. to be tried in December Court next ensuing, the date thereof or sooner if the deft. be here; in Sept. Court the deft. not being here the cause is referred until the next Court; in November Court the deft. not being here the cause is referred until the next Court."

P. 62:
" 8 & 9 of Nov. 1681.

Henry Bowman, plf. } An action of Debt.
Joseph Browne, deft. }

Jurymen {
Alexander Draper   William ffootcher
Daniel Brown   John Smith
William Emitt   John Long
Simon Psawling
}

In Sept. Court the deft. being out of the Government and his Attorney, Capt. John Avery being sick petitioned the Court for a reference; the Court therefore granted the deft. a reference until the next Court; in November Court the plf. declares that the defendant stands indebted unto him in 1000 lb. of tobacco; the deft. pleads that he had satisfied the Sheriff for that debt and craved a jury to try the cause; and after it was debated on both sides, the jury went out and brought in their verdict, that they find that the deft. had paid and satisfied the 1000 lb. tobacco by Capt. Avery engaging for the payment of it and therefore find for the deft. with one shill. damages and costs of suit. The Court passed judgment accordingly according to the verdict of the jury. Alias Execution."

P. 68:
" 8, 9, Nov. 1681.

Thomas Howard & }
   Wright Howard, plfs. } An action of Trespass.
Nathaniel Walker, deft. }

	Norton Claypoole	Alexander Draper
	Henry Bowman	James Welles
Jurymen	John Smith	Halmanus Wiltbank
	William flootcher	Robert Bracey
	John Hill	Samuel Gray
	Thomas Pinder	Daniell Browne

118:003

In Sept. Court the deft. being out of the Government and
his Attorney, Capt. John Avery, being sick, petitioned the
Court for a reference; the Court, therefore, granted the deft.
a reference until the next Court; the plfs. declare that the
deft. committed a trespass on his land; the deft. denied it;
and both plf. and deft. agreed to put it to a jury, before
whom the business was debated, after which the jury went
out and brought in their verdict, expressed in these words:
the jury finds for the deft. and gives him twelve pounds
damages. The Court order judgment to be entered according to the verdict of the jury. Alias Execution."

P. 63:
"8, 9, Nov. 1681.
Henry Bowman, plf. ⎫
Joseph Browne and ⎬ An action of Debt."
   Andrew Depree, defts. ⎭
Capt. John Avery, Attorney for Deft.

" Joseph Browne & ⎫
   Andrew Depree, plffs. ⎬
Henry Brown, deft. ⎭
Action withdrawn by order of plf's Atty."

P. 64:
"8, 9, Nov. 1681.
Andrew Depre, plf. ⎫
              ⎬ An action of the Case."
Thomas Denison, deft, ⎭
Capt. John Avery, Attorney for Deft.

3

Ibid. :

"Capt. John Avery, plf. } An action of the case
Benj. Coudrey, deft.   } upon attachment.
Plf. non suit for default of an appearance."

P. 65.   Same date :
"Francis Gunby, plf.   } An action of the Case.
Capt. John Avery, deft. }   (Debt.)
Judg. for plf."

P. 68 :
"13 Dec. 1681.
Capt. John Avery, plf. } Plea upon the case.
Peter Grundyk, deft.   }
Referred until next Court."

P. 70.   Same date :
"Capt. John Avery, plf. } An action of the case.
Ben. Coudrey, deft.   }
Referred until next Court."

Same page and date :
"Capt. John Avery, plf. } An action of the case.
ffrancis Gunby, deft.   }
Verdict for plff."

Same page and date :
"Capt. Avery, plf. } An action of the case.
ffra. Gumby, deft. }
Nonsuit."

P. 75 :
"10 Jan. 168½.
Capt. John Avery, plf. } Plea upon the case.
Peter Grundyk, deft.   }
Nonsuit."

P. 76. Same date:

"Capt. John Avery, plf. }
Benjamin Coudrey, deft. } Case.
Verd. for plf."

P. 91:

"14, 15, March 168½.
Capt. John Avery, plf. }
Richard Patte, deft. } Case.
Withdrawn."

P. 129:
1682.

"Coppie. William Penn Esqr Proprietary & Gov-
7th 9ber. ernor of Pennsylvania, New Castle, St.
Jones, Whore Kill, als New Deale with
their proper Libertys:
I doe in the King's name hereby Constitute & Authorize
you Luke Wattson, William Clark, John Roades, John
Auery and Halmanias Wiltbank or any three of you to be
Justices of the Peace And Court of Judicature for the
County of Whore Kills als New Deal, to Act in the said
Imployment and Trust for the preservation of the peace and
Justices of the prouience. Hereby willing and charging all
persons within the said Limits to take notice hereof. An
accordingly to yield you all due and Just obedience in the
discharge of your said Trust. And this Comixon to be of
force for the space of one whole year from the date hereof
or untill further order. Giuen under my hand and Seal In
New Castle this 7th day of November 1682.

Wm PENN

To My Loving ffriends
    LUKE WATTSON
    Wm CLARK
    JOHN RHOADES
    JOHN AUERY
    HALMANIAS WILTBANK"

P. 162:

" 9, 10, 11, ⅿᵒ/₁₁ 1682.

The Court order and appoint John Roades, Norton Claypoole, William footcher and John depree Appraisers of the Estate of Capt. John Auery, deceased."

P. 172:

"Upon petition of Sarah Auery, Admx. of Capt. John Auery, deceased, the Court remit a fine against decedent."

P. 204 :

" 31, 6 mo, 1683.

In re appraisement of Estate of Capt. Jno. Auery, dec'd."

P. 243 :

" 11ᵗʰ 1ˢᵗ mo. 1684.

Mathew Scarborow, plf.
Robert Clifton, marrying
    the Relix & Admx. of Capt. } Case.
    John Avery.
Nonsuit."

P. 11, Nᵒ 2:

" 11ᵗʰ 1ˢᵗ mo 1684.

William Roades, plf.
Estate of George Andrews } Case upon
    in the custody of Robert } Attachment.
    Clifton, deft.
Suit withdrawn. Sarah mentioned as wife of Robert Clifton."

P. 12, Nᵒ 2:

" Eodie.

Mathew Scarborow, plf.
Robt. Clifton, marrying
    the Relix & Admx. of } Case.
    Capt. John Avery, deft.
Nonsuit."

Sussex County Court Record. (Old Docket in possession of the Pa. His. Soc.)

P. 46:

" Court held 12ᵗʰ 6 mo. 1684.

Thomas Hodgkins petitioned agst. the Estate of Capt. John Avery for being indebted to the Estate of Halmanus Wiltbank, seventeen hundred and ninety pounds of tobacco and one hundred and ninety five pounds of pork due, upon account for which 1798 lb. tobacco and 195 lb. pork he craves order of this Court for, with costs. Thomas Clifton and Sarah his wife, who is the relict and administratrix of the Estate of Capt. John Avery, do plead they have never had a copy of the said account and do believe they may have a discharge to part of the sd. account or that they may have another account agst. it; upon which, the Court orders the petitioner to deliver unto Thomas Clifton a copy of the account."

" Return of Proprietory Quit Rents in Lewes and Rehoboth [Hundreds] of Sussex County on Delaware, 18 of 12 mo. 170⅝."

P. 2:

" Richard Hinman—300 acres on King's Creek.

Refuses to account.

Part of 800 acres called 'Avery's Rest,' granted by Pat. from Sʳ Edmd. Andros, dat. 15 Jany. 1675, to John Avery, who sold about 200 to Jno. Depre whose son John holds it. The other 600 he left to his 2 daughters, Mary and Jemima. Mary intermarried with Hercules Sheppard and R. Hinman married her, being his widow. Capt. Avery died 1682."

"John Morgan, 300 acres.

Nothing appears.

The other moiety of the 600 acres left by Capt. Avery to his daughter Jemima who intermarried with John Morgan; he married his wife about 7 years ago."

P. 10:

"George Marriner, 300 acres.

Taken up by Capt. Avery who sold it to Jno. Sheppard, whose attorney sold it to Marriner. It was taken up about 1680.

900 acres granted by Sir Edmund Andros, by patent dated 20 Aug. 1679 to Robt. Hignat & Jno. Crew. Jno. immediately sold his interest to R. Hignat."

Deed Book A, p. 74, Georgetown, Del.:

"John and Jemima Morgan, plaintiffs; Richard and Mary Hinman, defendants. Griffiths Jones, attorney for the former; James Thomas, attorney for the defendants.

Declaration was read against the defendants for £200 damages, for gainsaying to make partition according to law of a certain 800 acres of land lying upon Rehoboth Bay, belonging to said Mary and Jemima, the late inheritance of Capt. John Avery, their father, deceased. A copy of the record with manifesto to possession of one of the said messuages given by Capt. Avery in his lifetime to Hercules Shepard, joined in marriage with the said Mary, and the said Capt. Avery in his lifetime often saying, and upon his death-bed, that his daughter Mary should have the land, which several members of the Court having also heard the said Capt. Avery declare the same; therefore, upon the petition of the said Hercules Shepard, the Court passed judgment that the land doth belong to the same petitioner and to his heirs and assigns.

The plaintiff's attorney pleaded that the Court could not make title to lands, nor no one else, except Captain Avery had done it by deed and writing under hand and seal, acknowledged according to law in his lifetime.

The Defendants Attorney pleaded that the said Hercules had been at great charge and trouble in building upon and improving the said land for the good of his children, which is a thing of great moment and should be taken notice of, as that they have had sixteen or seventeen years quiet possession.

With some other pros and cons, the case was left to the jury which found for the plaintiffs, saving the improvements of Hercules Shepard to the defendants. Thomas Fenwick, foreman. The Court accepted the verdict and ordered a jury of twelve men to meet at said plantation on Saturday, 18 June 1698, to view and appraise the improvements of said Hercules Shepard and to make return of the same valuation and appraisement at next assembling of Court. Issued out the 17th instant."

Deed Book A, p. 217, Georgetown, Del. :
" John and Jemima Morgan, at a Court held 9 June last (1698), did recover judgment of Court by verdict of the jury against Richard and Mary Hinman for partition and division of two messuages or plantations of 800 acres left to be divided equally according to the true and equal worth and value of the whole according to the said verdict of improvements of Hercules Shepard, deceased, to the use of his children by the said Mary. The Court ordered a jury of twelve freeholders, who, 28 June 1698, by William Dyer, Sheriff, gave unto the Court in writing the following : The Jury whose names are here subscribed have valued and appraised the land and plantation, formerly belonging unto Capt. John Avery, now in dispute between Richard Hinman and Mary, his wife, and John Morgan and Jemima, his wife, coheirs of the same John Avery. That part of the land as now divided with the plantation where the said John Avery formerly lived and the other half where Hercules Shepard

formerly lived is valued at £380. Our verdict is that whichsoever of them hath the plantation and dividend of land as
now divided and where the said Capt. Avery lived shall pay
to the other 100£ current money. And whichsoever of
them shall have the other division where Hercules Shepard
formerly lived shall pay the improvements as appraised by
the former appointed Jury. Witness our hand 23 June
1698.

Thomas Fenwick	James Askue	Thomas Besant
John Meirs	Henry Stretcher	Peter Lewis
John Paynter	Richard Paynter	Cornelius Wiltbank
John Barker	Robert Barton	Richard Williams
	William Dyer.	

John and Jemima Morgan being present acknowledge
themselves agreed within themselves for choice in the
premises."

Deed Book F, fol. 21 :
"Deed dated Aug. 7, 1720, Recorded Aug. 7, 1722.
Henry Draper of Sussex County, and Sarah his wife, one
of the granddaughters of John Avery, deceased, Convey
to Richard Hinman Esq. ¼ portion of 800 acres confirmed
by patent unto John Avery, 15 Jan. 1675, called 'Avery's
Rest,' lying upon Rehoboth ; and in same deed it is recited
that said John Avery died intestate, leaving issue five children, viz : Mary, Elizabeth, Sarah, Jemina and John, since
deceased, and that the said Sarah intermarried with John
Kipshaven and had issue Sarah Draper and that Sarah the
mother being dead, the said ¼ int. doth belong to Sarah,
wife of H. Draper."

Robert Clifton, the second husband of Sarah, the widow
of Captain John Avery, was quite a prominent man in Sussex County. He was appointed one of the judges of the
Court April 9, 1686, and appears in office as late as 1696.
(See the Court Records of that period.)

There was a younger Robert Clifton who married Anne, dau. of Thos. Fenwick, but whether he was the son of the former by his marriage with Capt. Avery's widow I have not ascertained.

Sarah Clifton appears upon the Court Record May 5, 1703, as widow of Robert Clifton. Upon the death of the former Robert Clifton, the widow married, third, Thomas Clifton, who was a Prov. Councillor, 1690. (Col. Rec., Vol. I, p. 324.) I do not know what relation he was to either of the aforementioned Robert Cliftons.

Capt. John Avery left issue by his wife Sarah :

2. Mary.
3. Elizabeth.
4. Sarah.
5. Jemima.
6. John.

II. 2. MARY AVERY, dau. of Capt. John Avery (1), m. first, Hercules Shepheard ; second, Richard Hinman.

Old Court Docket of Sussex Co. in possession Pa. His. Soc.

" 14, 15, March 1681, The Court grant unto Hecules Sheepard 300 acres ; warrant given him the 16ᵗʰ."

" List of Officers of the Colonies on the Delaware and the Province of Pennsylvania, 1614–1776." (Pa. Ar., Sec. Ser.)

P. 664 :
Hercules Shepherd appointed a Justice of the Peace 1683.

The old Court Docket of Sussex County in possession of the Pa. His. Soc.

P. 207 :
Hercules Shepherd present as a judge of the Court 1683.

P. 214 :
Ditto.

P. 228 :
Ditto.

P. 239 :
Ditto. The signature of " Hercules Shepheard," subscribed
to a Declaration of Fidelity to the Proprietary by the Judges
of the Court. His name is distinctly spelled "Shepheard,"
although references to him and the names of his descendants, named after him, appear spelled either "Shephard,"
"Sheppard," or "Shepherd."

It is very difficult to give the numbers of the pages of the
references in the old Docket before mentioned, as it is not
numbered regularly. References, therefore, must be sought
according to the dates given.

Hercules Shepheard sits as a Judge of the Orphans'
Court, 2, 7 mo., 1684. (See also Scharf's "His. of Del.,"
p. 1211.)

"List of Officers of the Colonies, etc.," p. 667; "Duke
of York's Laws," p. 495.
Hercules Shepherd, Member from Sussex of the Assembly
of the Three Lower Counties, 1684.

Hercules Shepheard acknowledges sale of land to Norton
Claypoole for use of daughter Mary, 10, 1 mo., 1685. (I do
not know whose daughter is meant.)

Richard Hinman and his wife, Admx. of Hercules Shepheard, appear in Court May 9, 1706.

Orphans' Court held May 9, 1706, Richard Hinman and
Mary his wife, Admx. of Hercules Shepherd dec'd., filed an
account.

Hercules Shephard appears as one of the Overseers of
Highways Oct. 5 & 6, 1687.

Orphans' Ct. held Mar. 4, 1706, Richard Hinman, in right of his wife Mary, Admx. of the Estate of Hercules Shepherd, deceased.

Hercules Shepherd fined 10/ for non-attendance as a juryman Dec. 7, 1694.

"Orphans' Ct. held Sep. 2, 1707. Richard Hinman appeared in relation to the Estate of Hercules Shephard deceased, and Comfort Shepheard, daughter of Hercules Shepheard acknowledged herself satisfied in her father's estate."

" Civil List of Officers &c."
Richard Hinman mentioned as a Justice of the Peace 1719.

Richard Hinman Commissioned a Judge of the Supreme Court by William Keith, April 13, 1720. (Record Book D, p. 384.)

Book D, p. 64 :
Mary, wife of Richard Hinman, gives to her son John Hinman, from natural love and affection, by deed of gift, land belonging to John Avery, her father. Dated May 3, 1709. Recorded Aug. 9, 1709.

Mary (2), by her husband Hercules Shepheard, had issue :
    7. Sarah.
    8. Comfort, m. first, —— Prettyman; m. second, Simon Kollock, from which marriage the writer descends. For the descendants, see " Kollock Genealogy."
    9. Alice, m. Col. Jacob Kollock. For descendants, see " Kollock Genealogy."
    10. John.

Mary (2), by her husband Richard Hinman, had issue :
    11. John.
    12. Richard.

III. 11. JOHN HINMAN, son of Richard Hinman and Mary Avery Shephard (2), his wife, m. Mary ——.

Will Book A, Georgetown, Del.:
Will of John Hinman, dated Aug. 27, 1724, probated Sep. 23, 1727. Mentions wife Mary, two sons, John and Richard, and daughter Elizabeth. He also mentions his brother Richard Hinman, John Roades and Philip Russell, Overseers.

John Hinman (11) and Mary his wife had issue:
    13. John.
    14. Richard.
    15. Elizabeth.

III. 12. RICHARD HINMAN, son of Richard Hinman and Mary (2) his wife, m. ——.

Will Book A, p. 373, Georgetown, Delaware. Will of Richard Hinman:
"In the name of God Amen The thirtieth day of January one thousand and seven Hundred and forty one, I Richard Hinman of the County of Sussex Upon Delaware being sick and weak of body but of good sound disposing mind and memory praised be God for the same and knowing the uncertainty of all things on Earth and being desirious to settle things in order and dispose of that Estate which God of his Goodness far above my deserts hath been pleased to bless me with do make ordain constitute and appoint this my Last will and testament to be in manner and form following.

I give and bequeath my soul unto the hand of Almighty God who gave it me and my body to the Earth to receive such decent Christianlike Burial as by my Executrix and Executor hereafter named shall be thought meet and convenient in sure and certain hopes of a resurection in and through the Merits and Mediation of my blessed Lord and Saviour Jesus Christ.

I give and bequeath unto my daughter Naomy Roades widow of John Roades deed., the Land and plantation whereon I now dwell containing three hundred and thirty five acres of land and Marsh taken up and pattented in my own name as pr the pattent being thereunto had may more fully appear with all the Housing and Improvements thereunto belonging with and Island of land and Marsh lying in Rehoboth Bay partly adjoining to the afsd. land commonly called and known by the name of the Horse Island to her and her heirs forever.

I give and bequeath unto my two grandsons Hinman Roads and John Roads Sons of my above sd. daughter Naomy all other my land and plantation which I purchased from Daniel Coe and others in this County or elsewhere with my housing and lots in and near Lewis Town to be equally divided between my afsd. two grand sons in quality and quantity to be posest thereof when they arrive to the age of twenty one years or day of marriage which shall first happen to them and their heirs forever. And in case either of the above sd. two grandsons should die before they arrive to lawful age or day of marriage as aforesd. then the survivor to enjoy the whole land and housing as aforesd. to him and his heirs forever. I further will and order that all of my estate consisting either in negroes gold silver paper money household goods cattle sheep horses hogs or any other merchandise or moveables whatsoever in this County or elsewhere to be divided into three equal shares one full third part thereof I give and bequeath unto my afsd. daughter Naomy Roades and her heirs forever; one full third part thereof I give and bequeath unto my grandson Hinman Roades and his heirs forever. And the other third part I give and bequeath unto my grandson John Roades and his heirs forever.

Lastly, I make and ordain my aforesd. daughter Naoma Roades and my friend Cornelius Wiltbank Esq. Executrix and Executor of this my last will and testament, thereby revoking all other will or wills by me heretofore made either by word of mouth or in writing. In witness whereof

I have hereunto set my hand and Seal the day and year first within written.

RICH⁰ HINMAN [SEAL]

Signed Sealed published pronounced and declared by the afsd. Richard Hinman to be his last will and testament in the presence of us

JOHN BICKNALL
JOHN MOLLESTON JOHN LEWIS"

This will was probated the 13ᵗʰ of August, 1742.

Col. Rec., Vol. III, p. 259:
Richard Hinman commissioned a Justice of the Peace for Sussex Co.

P. 270:
Apr. 20, 1727, again commissioned.

Richard Hinman (12) and his wife had issue:
    16. Naomy.

IV. 16. NAOMY, dau. of Richard Hinman (12), m. John Roades and had issue:
    17. Hinman. (See will of Richard Hinman (12).)
    18. John. (Ditto.)

II. 4. SARAH AVERY, daughter of Capt. John Avery (1) and Sarah his wife, m. John Kipshaven.
Will of John Kipshaven on file at Georgetown, Delaware.

P. 664:
John Kipshaven mentioned as a Justice of the Peace, 1681.

"List of Officers, etc.," p. 667; Col. Rec., Vol. I, p. 48.
John Kipshaven Member of Assembly from Sussex 2, 2 mo. 1682–3.
(For further reference to John Kipshaven and his wife Sarah (4), see account of Capt. John Avery (1).)

John Kipshaven and Sarah his wife had issue :
19. Sarah, m. Henry Draper. (See Capt. John Avery (1).)

II. 5. JEMIMA, dau. of Capt. John Avery (1), m. John Morgan. (See Capt. John Avery (1).)

II. 6. JOHN AVERY, son of Capt. John Avery (1), d. young, according to the letter of Daniel Nunez, a copy of which is herein inserted.

The original letter, of which the following is a copy, is in possession of Mr. Charles Swift Riché Hildeburn. Daniel Nunez, the writer, married Hannah, daughter, of Col. Jacob Kollock and Alice Shephard, referred to in the letter, which is addressed to John Swift, who married the said Hannah's sister, Magdalen Kollock. (See "Kollock Genealogy.")

"SIR :

I have after a long search amongst the old records found most of the papers that is necessary for us towards the recovery of our part of the land that belonged to the late Mᵗˢ Alice Kollock, but as there is [word torn out] papers at Philadelphia and New Castle which [word torn out] be necessary for us to have as we must depend altogether upon copys as the originals are out of our possession and the tenants in possession are determined not to give up any part of the land until it is legally recovered from them for which reason I shall be obliged to you to make search in the Surveyor general's office in Philadᵃ for the surveys & returns of the following tracts of land and send a copy of them down to me, viz, one granted to Capᵗ John Avery the 9ᵗʰ April 1679 for 800 acres called Avery's rest also a grant or resurvey of an island laying adjoyning to the afsᵈ tract granted the 16ᵗʰ April 1682 (but I believe this island was afterwards secured by Hercules Shepard surveyed and Patented in his own name as Avery died some short time afterwards) another tract called Martin Vinyard or black walnut neck granted & Patented to Henry Strecher which he afterwards assigned

over to Avery there is one or two more tracts Avery had a
right in but how they have been transferred from his heirs
or how he came by them I cannot at present say. I want
also the survey and return of a grant that was made to Hurcules Shepard the 16 March 1682 for 300 ˢ but if it should
be for any lands on the South East side of Indian river I
have [word torn out] use for it as I have the original Patent
for all the [word torn out] he held on that side of the
river. but should you in your searching find any more surveys & returns of land made to either Avery or Shepard
please to take notice of them and send me what they are
for and I will let you know whether they will be of service
to me or not.

    As you Sir may want to know how we claim under Avery
I will just give you a short state of our descent from him
viz. Avery died intestate and left issue four daughters and
one son to wit Mary, Elizabeth, Sarah, Jemima & John the
son died a minor Hercules Shepard intermarried with Mary
by whome he had four children to wit Sarah, Comfort, Alice
& John which son died an infant Shepard died also intestate
And under Alice we claim. I would have been more particular in informing you of what became of Avery's other
children and of what part of the lands we claim, but I have
had a very severe return of my disorder in my stomach that
for this eight or ten days past I have not been well able to
write as much as is contained in this paper had that not
been the case I should have gone up with John Woods to
[word torn out] some affairs I have there which I cannot
well do without going up. I have had Mr McKean's second
opinion on Mr Phillips will he says he has carefully considered Mr Chew's case and confesses at first now they appear
to be cases in point that is in favour of the limitation over
but upon a careful comparison of them and the case then
before him there is a manifest difference for the remainder
man was to take immediately upon the death of the first
devisee without leaving a child *then living* But in default
of issue of H. N. it is given to her next of kin &c. So that
the principal & interest is not to go over at her death with-

Fitzgibbony & S. Green & Rod a very strong case ask
stays and do conclude that if the Principal
don't go to Hannah, he cannot see what
service it can be to an Ed.s of Mr Phillips
who must always pay intent for it, is so that
you see he still returns his former opinion
I am hearty & T. D with waiting, and do
not you will in reading it so for whatever
I will conclude

Hannah is well and desires a tender of
L. L. P. Timmer MMM Little. D. P. O.

over to Avery there is one or two more tracts Avery had a right in but how they have been transferred from his heirs or how he came by them I cannot at present say. I want also the survey and return of a grant that was made to Hurcules Shepard the 16 March 1682 for 300 ª but if it should be for any lands on the South East side of Indian river I have [word torn out] use for it as I have the original Patent for all the [word torn out] he held on that side of the river. but should you in your searching find any more surveys & returns of land made to either Avery or Shepard please to take notice of them and send me what they are for and I will let you know whether they will be of service to me or not.

As you Sir may want to know how we claim under Avery I will just give you a short state of our descent from him viz. Avery died intestate and left issue four daughters and one son to wit Mary, Elizabeth, Sarah, Jemima & John the son died a minor Hercules Shepard intermarried with Mary by whome he had four children to wit Sarah, Comfort, Alice & John which son died an infant Shepard died also intestate And under Alice we claim. I would have been more particular in informing you of what became of Avery's other children and of what part of the lands we claim, but I have had a very severe return of my disorder in my stomach that for this eight or ten days past I have not been well able to write as much as is contained in this paper had that not been the case I should have gone up with John Woods to [word torn out] some affairs I have there which I cannot well do without going up. I have had Mr McKean's second opinion on Mr Phillips will he says he has carefully considered Mr Chew's case and confesses at first now they appear to be cases in point that is in favour of the limitation over but upon a careful comparison of them and the case then before him there is a manifest difference for the remainder man was to take immediately upon the death of the first devisee without leaving a child *then living* But in default of issue of H. N. it is given to her next of kin &c. So that the principal & interest is not to go over at her death with-

out issue (then living) but after a general failure of issue of H. which would tend to a perpetuity and be too remote and therefore void. The following are the cases he refers to 2 Vent 349 sid 450 Pollexfen from fol. 24 to 44 Fitzgibbons 68 Green & Rod a very strong case as he says and so concludes that if the principal dont go to Hannah he cannot see what service it can be to an Ex^r of Mr Phillips who must always pay interest for it so that you see he still retains his former opinion.

I am hartily tired with writing and I [doubt] not you will in reading it for which [reason] I will conclude.

Hannah is well and desires a tender of her love to you Mrs Swift and famely.

With Sir
Your assured friend,
and Humble Servt
DAN^l NUNEZ
May 23: 1772.

JOHN SWIFT ESQ."

A *fac-simile* copy of the foregoing is inserted in this work.

Index

www.ingramcontent.com/pod-product-compliance
Lightning Source LLC
Chambersburg PA
CBHW021227260626
47172CB00002B/638